Natalie's Hair was Wild!

BY Laura Freeman

Clarion Books | Houghton Mifflin Harcourt | Boston New York

CLARION BOOKS
3 Park Avenue
New York, New York 10016

Copyright © 2018 by Laura Freeman

Clarion Books is an imprint of Houghton Mifflin Harcourt Publishing Company.
www.hmhco.com

The illustrations in this book were produced digitally.
The text was set in Andy Std.

Library of Congress Cataloging-in-Publication Data is available.
ISBN 978-1-328-66195-1

Manufactured in China
SCP 10 9 8 7 6 5 4 3 2 1
4500673600

To Lynne, for believing in me

Natalie's hair was wild.
It seemed to have a mind of its own.
It couldn't be tamed by a comb or a pick
or restrained by barrettes or a clip.

Her hair could escape from a scrunchie.
It was tangled and frizzy,
and each day it got wilder.
But Natalie didn't care.

One day some birds moved in.
Natalie's hair made a fine nest.

She didn't care.

Then a frog jumped in.

Natalie just let her hair get wilder.

An owl and a fox arrived next.
An ostrich thought
it was the perfect place
to hide his face.
Natalie didn't care.

Soon a zebra was living there.
A giraffe and an elephant too!
Natalie still didn't care.

She didn't mind
the wildebeest or rabbits.

There was even a tiger!
Natalie's hair was really wild!

GRRRR

And those animals were loud!
They snorted and growled.
They honked and chirped.
They squeaked and burped.
They never stopped!
Natalie didn't care.

tweet!.

squeak!

HONK

squeak!

Achoo!

chirp

tweet!

BURP!

snort

But the wild sounds went on all day and all night.
Soon Natalie could no longer ignore them.
"I've had enough. I want these animals out of here!
They won't let me sleep, and they're just plain rude."

Hiccup

screech!

cough

tweet!

It was time to take action.

Natalie knew it would be a big job.

Those animals were all tangled up in her hair.

So she called in professionals from the zoo

and the fire department, too!

First they removed the zebra and the giraffe.

Then they coaxed out the fox and the rabbits.

They caught the tiger . . .

. . . and told the owl who-o-o they were.

They cleared them all out—every last one.

And when they were done,
they used their hoses to
wash Natalie's hair.

They raked through the knots
and trimmed her hair
with huge hedge scissors.
It really was a big job!

When they finally finished,
Natalie was relieved.
She understood
that the hair on your head
is no place for a zoo.

She faithfully brushed it
and combed it
and washed it.
She kept it neat . . .

. . . for at least a week.